Summary: A small boy visits the Georgia Aquarium for his
birthday where he enjoys seeing the many incredible aquatic creatures
and also soaks up some new ideas about
the value of giving to others.

ISBN
International Standard Book Number
distributed by R.R. Bowker company
1-930897-16-2

A GIVING TAIL ~~TALE~~ TALE

BY CLEVE WILLCOXON

ILLUSTRATED BY BILL MAYER

His father called, "Wake up, Davey! Wake up, I say!
Remember we're going to the Aquarium today!"
Davey's one eye popped open. And then the other.
This was an eye popping day unlike any other.
"I'm going to the Aquarium!" He yelled and he screamed.
It's the birthday present of which he had dreamed.
His real birthday wasn't until Tuesday,
But today was his big trip – it would be a doozy!

Davey liked toys and playing in parks,
But the rest of the time Davey thought about sharks.
He liked their sharp teeth and the fins on their backs,
The way that they swim and the way they attack!

"Davey!" His mom cried, "Before we go….
Your Giving Basket is empty you know.
Go through your toys. You have so many.
We'll give some to children who don't have any."

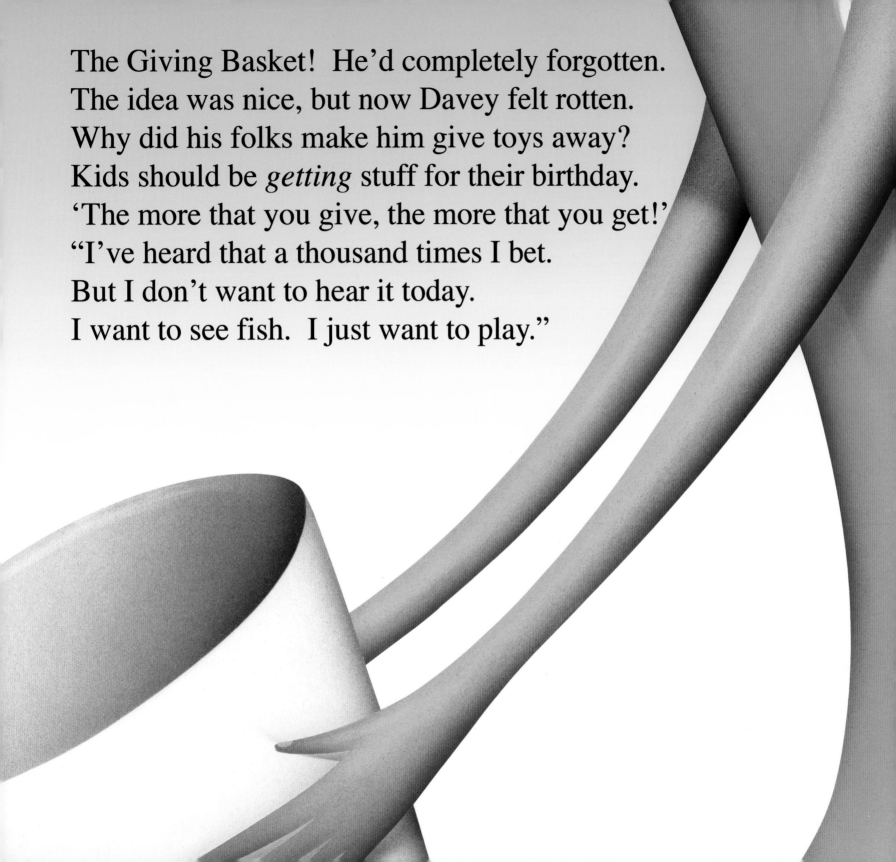

The Giving Basket! He'd completely forgotten.
The idea was nice, but now Davey felt rotten.
Why did his folks make him give toys away?
Kids should be *getting* stuff for their birthday.
'The more that you give, the more that you get!'
"I've heard that a thousand times I bet.
But I don't want to hear it today.
I want to see fish. I just want to play."

At last they arrived for the big birthday trip.
"Wow! It looks like a gigantic ship!"
They stared at the Aquarium - eyes open wide.
What would it be like on the inside?

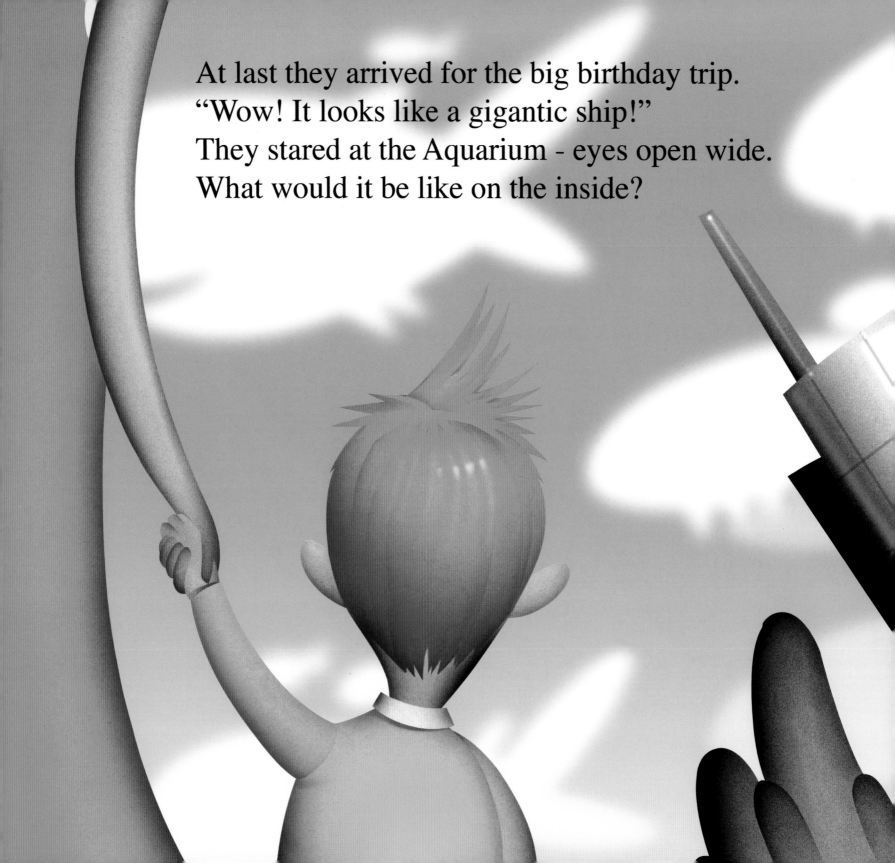

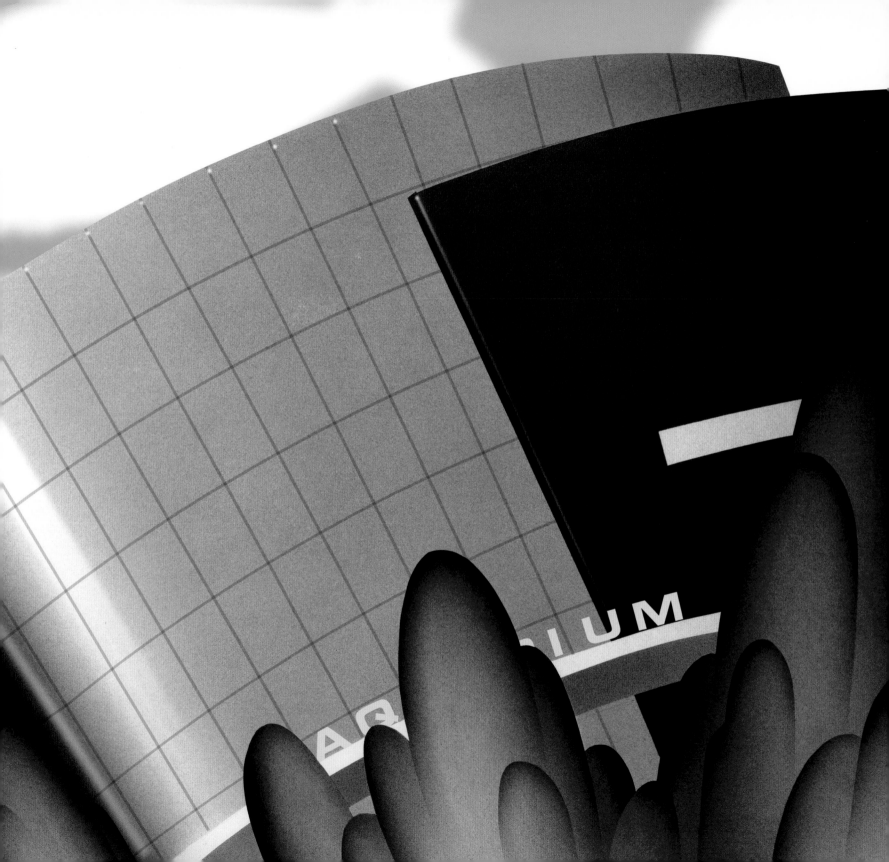

"Jumpin' jellyfish!" cried Davey. "It's beyond belief!
The Aquarium has its very own reef!
And look! Real waves keep the water in motion.
Whoa, this is just like it is in the ocean!"

The reef was a rainbow of tropical fish…
Puffers and Angels – everything you could wish.
"Where did they get all these things?" Davey wondered.
He could have stared until he turned one hundred.

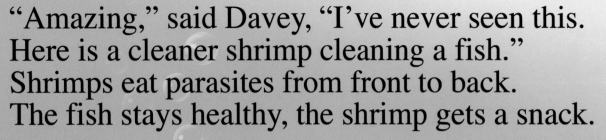

"Amazing," said Davey, "I've never seen this.
Here is a cleaner shrimp cleaning a fish."
Shrimps eat parasites from front to back.
The fish stays healthy, the shrimp gets a snack.

On to the tanks with live things you can touch,
Full of neat fish, crabs, rays and such.
As cool things go – this is right on the mark.
Davey even touched a real bonnethead shark!

Now to explore the world's fresh water rivers.
The piranhas' sharp teeth gave Davey the shivers.
Piranhas live in the Great Amazon.
Don't go swimming without steel swim-trunks on.

For sheer size the arapaima is the topper.
They can reach 15 feet! What a whopper!
But when they are babies, they live in the hollow—
of their parents' mouths! "Hey Dad, please don't swallow!"

Arapaima – Air-ah-pie-muh

"Awesome! Sea otters!" Davey said to his pop.
"They are the smartest, the neatest, the top!
Otters use rocks and hard things just like tools—
To break open shellfish to eat. That's so cool!"

"Penguins! Hey mom! Come here on the double!
You can see them close up from this clear plastic bubble.

They walk sorta funny and sound like a mule.
I never got a nature lesson like this at school."

Belugas are white whales from cold water seas
They grin and blow bubbles whenever they please.
Don't look at them sadly whatever you do,
They'll wonder why you are not grinning, too.

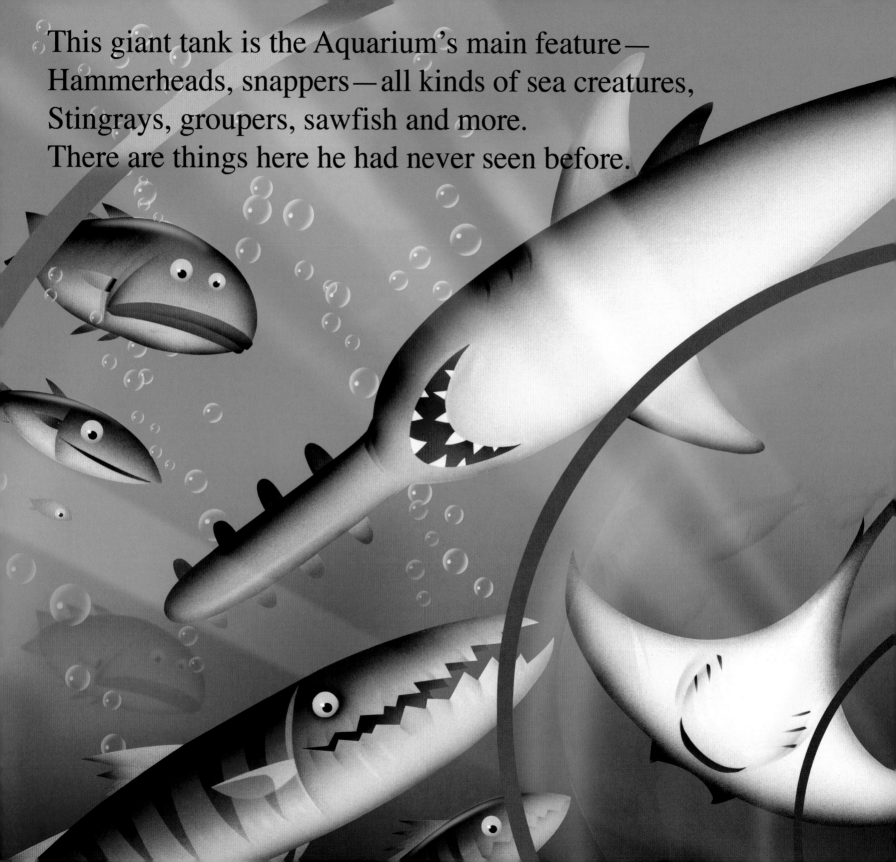

This giant tank is the Aquarium's main feature—
Hammerheads, snappers—all kinds of sea creatures,
Stingrays, groupers, sawfish and more.
There are things here he had never seen before.

Then Davey saw THEM! These huge spotted things!
White dots, brown bodies, fins wide as plane wings.
These are the largest fish in the whole sea—
Whale sharks way bigger than fish ought to be!

Whale sharks eat small stuff called krill and plankton.
They're gentle giants, it's a shame no one's thanked 'em.
And though they're sharks they would never hurt you—
Just stick out their fin and say "How do you do?"

It took quite a while for the sharks to swim past.
They're very, very big but they're not very fast.
It's lucky they eat things that also move slow.
You have to eat lots to get this big, you know.

"Look Davey, it's the people whose statues we viewed.
Should we say 'hi?' Not to speak would be rude."
"Let's meet them, dad. I want to say thanks.
For all of these fish in all of these tanks."

Davey said "Thank you!" to Bernie and Billi.
"But I have a question. I hope it's not silly.
Why did you give money to build all these things?
You could've bought squirt guns, candy, gold rings!"

"I love smiling people," Billi said. "And I see—
Whale shark-sized smiles on all of you three.
We had it to give so we gave it, and now—
We like to come back and hear people say, 'Wow!'"

Bernie said, "My mom had a saying I never forget,
'The more that you give, the more that you get.'
I try to remember it in all that I do,
And I've gotten a lot, Davey. I got to meet you!"

"Your mom is a lot like mine," said Davey.
"She says that same thing and it drives me crazy."
"Moms have lots of really smart things to say,"
Bernie said, "I think you'll understand that one day."

It was time to leave the Aquarium at last.
Why does something fun go by so fast?
Piranhas, sharks, otters, the reef, and the rest—
Davey couldn't decide which thing he liked best.

As Davey climbed into his bed for the night.
He thought about something that didn't feel right.
His thoughts made him throw off all of his covers,
He was thinking about caring and giving to others.

Later on, Davey's parents got quite a surprise,
It almost brought a tear to their eyes.
The Giving Basket, once so empty and clean,
Was filled with more toys than they'd ever seen.

The Marcus Institute is a charitable organization that works with children who have developmental disabilities, including autism and mental retardation. Highly trained professionals diagnose and treat children with a wide range of neurological problems, and carefully managed therapy teaches the children to thrive despite their disabilities. The Marcus Institute is committed to helping children realize their greatest potential, giving them and their families a higher quality of life. Their great work is funded largely by contributions made by the Marcus family and by people like the one reading this now.

THE END

Don't you think, since this is the end of the book, that the picture should be the fish's backside? You know, the tail-end of the fish.
That way, it would be the tail-end of the fish and the tale-end of the story. Wouldn't that have been cool? But the illustrator liked the way
the fish's front side looked much better than the fish's backside so he did this. So this is not the tail-end of the fish but it is the tale end
of the story. Anyway, it would have been cool.